BEE
AND
PUPPYCAT™
VOLUME
TWO

BEE AND PUPPYCAT™

BEE AND PUPPYCAT Volume Two, January 2016. Published by KaBOOM!, a division of Boom Entertainment, Inc. Based on "Bee and PuppyCat" © 2016 Frederator Networks, Inc. Originally published in single magazine form as BEE AND PUPPYCAT No. 5-8. ™ & © 2014, 2015 Frederator Networks, Inc. All rights reserved. KaBOOM!™ and the KaBOOM! logo are trademarks of Boom Entertainment, Inc., registered in various countries and categories. All characters, events, and institutions depicted herein are fictional. Any similarity between any of the names, characters, persons, events, and/or institutions in this publication to actual names, characters, and persons, whether living or dead, events, and/or institutions is unintended and purely coincidental. KaBOOM! does not read or accept unsolicited submissions of ideas, stories, or artwork.

A catalog record of this book is available from OCLC and from the KaBOOM! website, www.kaboom-studios.com, on the Librarians Page.

BOOM! Studios, 5670 Wilshire Boulevard, Suite 450, Los Angeles, CA 90036-5679. Printed in China. First Printing.

ISBN: 978-1-60886-776-9, eISBN: 978-1-61398-447-5

Created by

Natasha Allegri

"A Coffee Problem"
Written and Illustrated by
T. Zysk

"Served"
Written and Illustrated by
Meredith McClaren

"One Hit Wonder"
Written and Illustrated by
Chrystin Garland

"Bee and Puppycat in..."
Written and Illustrated by
Carey Pietsch

"The Claw Game"
Written and Illustrated by
Flynn Nicholls

"The Carnival"
Written and Illustrated by
Andrew Lorenzi

"Je Ne Sais Quoi"
Written and Illustrated by
Meredith McClaren

"Gardening"
Written and Illustrated by
Zachary Sterling
Colors by
Mad Rupert

"Book Quest"
Written and Illustrated by
Andrew Lorenzi

"Sick Day"
Written and Illustrated by
Megan Brennan

"Food"
Written and Illustrated by
Joy Ang
Letters by
Ashley Ang

"Pancoma"
Written and Illustrated by
T. Zysk

"Sweaters"
Written and Illustrated by
T. Zysk

"Bubbles"
Written and Illustrated by
Liz Fleming

"Snapshots"
Written and Illustrated by
David Calderon

"Tubberware"
Written and Illustrated by
Coleman Engle

"The Blues"
Written and Illustrated by
Reimena Yee

Cover Natasha Allegri • Collection Designer Kelsey Dieterich
Associate Editor Whitney Leopard • Editor Shannon Watters

With Special Thanks to Eric Homan, Fred Seibert and all of the classy folks at Frederator Studios.

"A Coffee Problem"
Written & Illustrated by
T. Zysk
Puppycat, I'm home!!
<What is that.>
Oh it's just a coffee.
I mean yeah it's artisan coffee and costs like 5 dollars a cup.
And yeah it's got chocolate and espresso in it so it's loaded with sugar and caffeine.
But I've got a handle on it.
slp
fmp
What?
I'm a young adult and I make my own life choices!
And then...

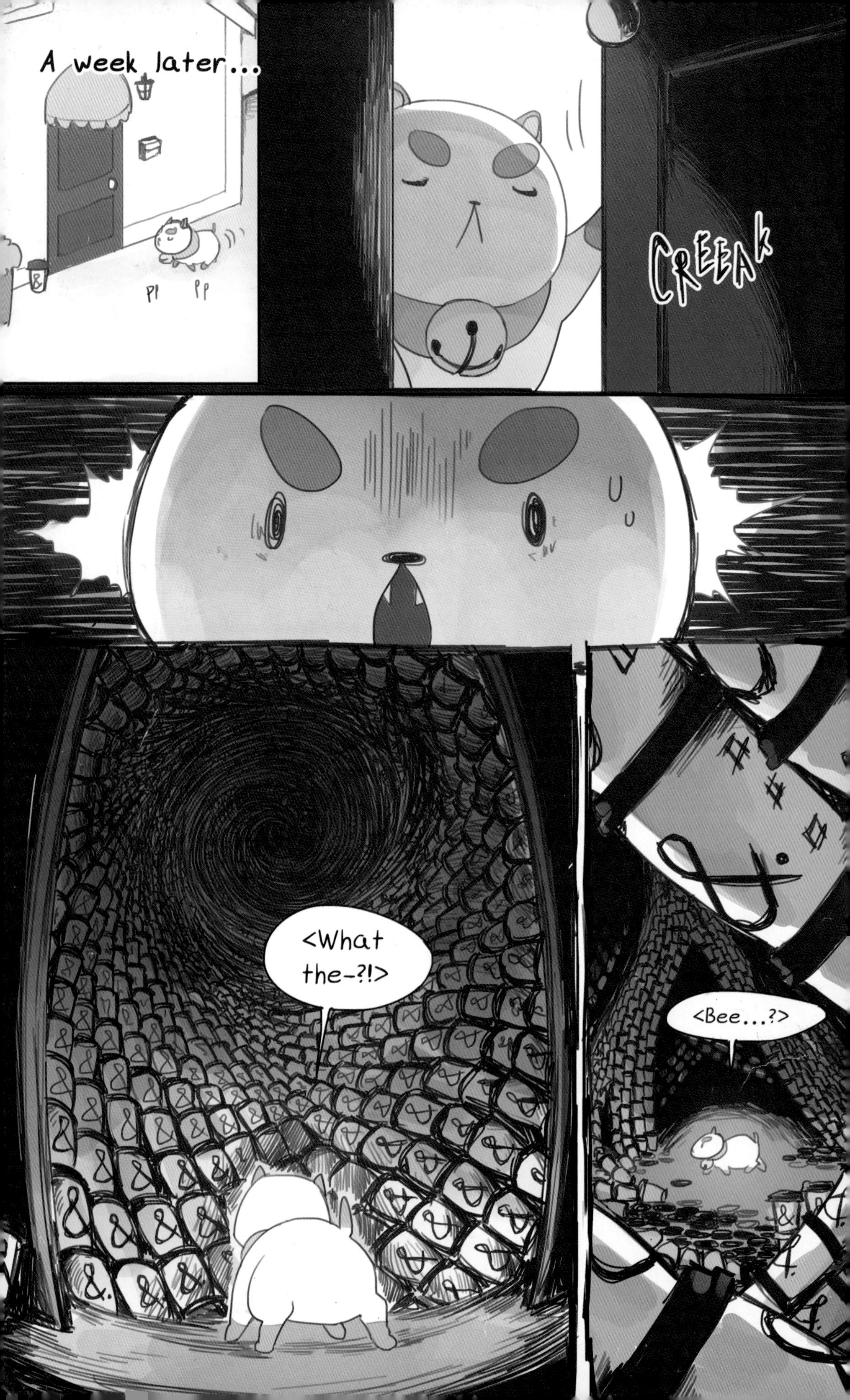
A week later...
pi pp
CREEAK
<What the-?!>
<Bee...?>

Puppycat...
I've been awake for 41 hours...
ENCYCLOPEDIA
and I've almost memorized all of the facts about parakeets...
No I need to learn this though...
Yoink
tuk
tuk
I'm a young adult and I...

SNRT
tug tug
WOOSHHHH
toss
THE NEXT DAY...
Puppycat! I'm-
thwakk
Hey!
Man you are so weird sometimes.
END

MAN, THIS STAGE WAS HARD TO BUILD, BUT TOTALLY WORTH IT. LOOK AT THIS CROWD!
< AND THEY HAVE SNACKS! >
OH, THANK GOODNESS YOU'RE HERE!
SLURP!
ONE HiT WONDER
WRITTEN AND ILLUSTRATED BY CHRYSTIN GARLAND
WE'RE IN THE MIDDLE OF OUR RADIANT QUEEN'S 600TH ALL NIGHT KARAOKE BIRTHDAY EXTRAVAGANZA!
THOUGH, BY THE LOOK OF THINGS, I DON'T THINK IT'S GOING TOO WELL...

MORE, MUSIC!
YES, YOUR MAJESTY!

I'M AFRAID WE'VE RUN OUT OF SONGS TO PLAY, YOUR MAJESTY --
-- BUT I'VE BEEN WORKING ON THIS NEW ONE ALL NIGHT LONG! I-I HOPE YOU LIKE IT...

OH WOW, HE'S SO AMAZING!!!

THIS IS ...
UNIMPRESSIVE!
SPLAT!

BROTHER, ARE YOU ALL RIGHT?
OF COURSE NOT.

I'VE FAILED AGAIN!
OUR QUEEN'S TASTE IN UNDERGROUND MUSIC IS TOO EXCEPTIONAL!!

SO, THIS JOB... IT DOESN'T INVOLVE DECAPITATION DOES IT?
NOT IF YOU PACIFY OUR LOVELY QUEEN WITH A SONG THAT IS BOTH UNIQUE AND PLEASING TO HER SQUISHY EARS!
SHE SEEMS... PICKY.
AS LONG AS YOU STAY AWAY FROM SPACE POP OR SPACE R&B, YOU'LL BE FINE.
< WHAT ABOUT COUNTRY? >
NOBODY LIKES COUNTRY.

HMM... STILL SEEMS PRETTY DANGEROUS.
ROCK, PAPER, SCISSORS?
< SOUNDS FAIR. >

SHOOT!

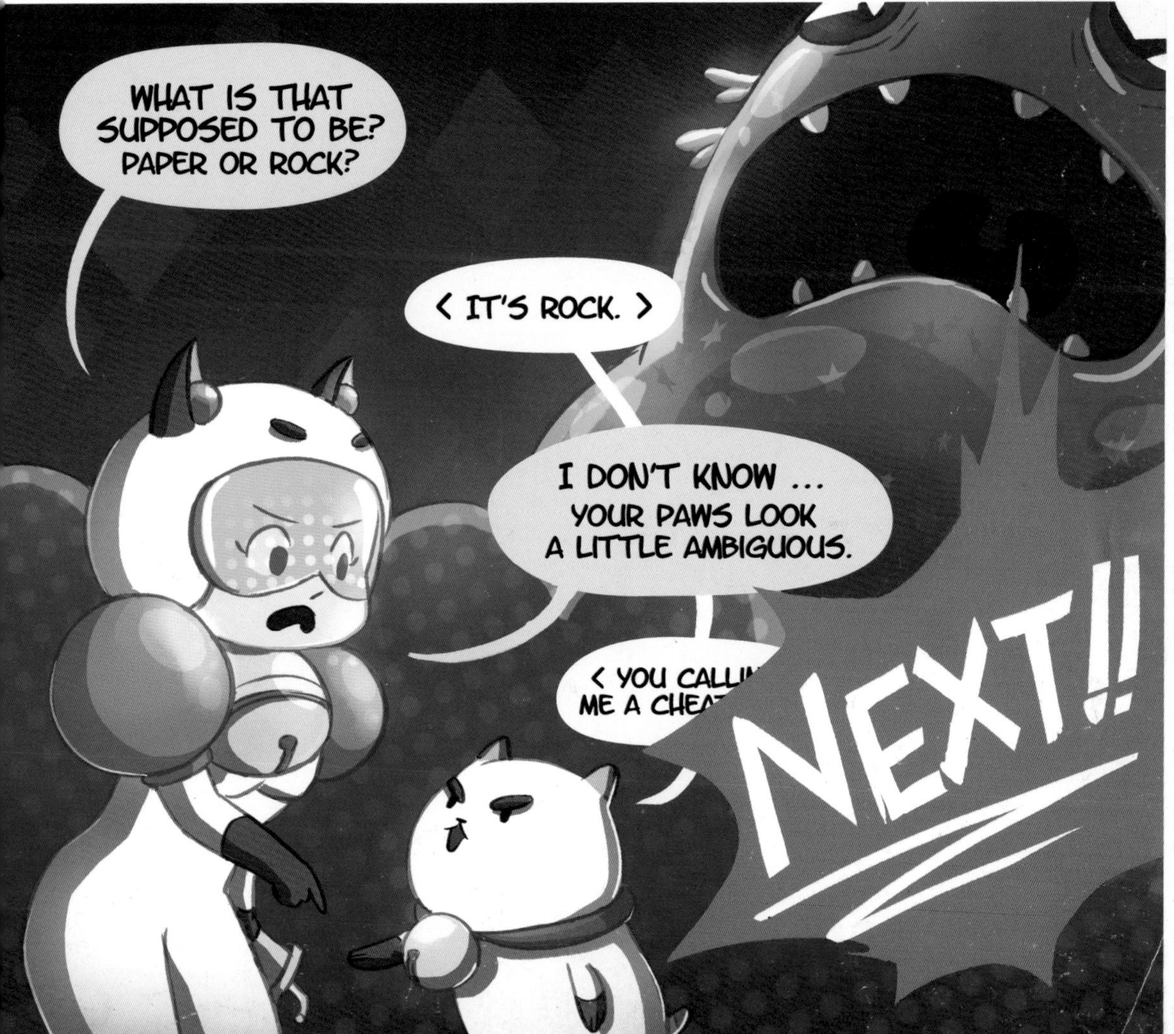
WHAT IS THAT SUPPOSED TO BE? PAPER OR ROCK?
< IT'S ROCK. >
I DON'T KNOW ... YOUR PAWS LOOK A LITTLE AMBIGUOUS.
< YOU CALLI ME A CHEA
NEXT!!

UM, BEFORE WE START...

I JUST WANT YOU ALL TO KNOW I'M NOT A TRAINED SINGER, BUT--

BURRRRRP!!

...EXCUSE ME.
< YOU BLEW IT! SHE'S GOING TO KILL US ALL! >

YOU CALL THAT MUSIC?

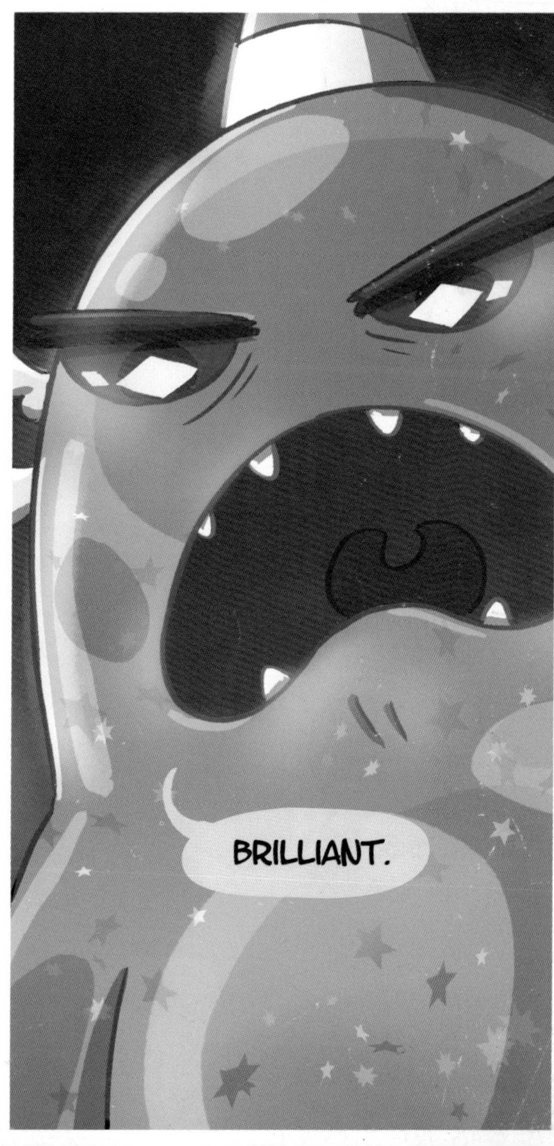
BRILLIANT.

WIKKY!
WIKKY!
ABSOLUTELY BRILLIANT!
WE SHALL PLAY THIS NEW MELODY FOR CENTURIES TO COME!
B-BURP!
B-BURP!
BELCH!
BELCH
HA HA HA!
GROSS.
BEELLCH!
THE END

"The Claw Game"
Written & Illustrated by
Flynn Nicholls
PUPPYCAT?
WHERE ARE YOU?

mew
PUPPYCAT!
HOW'D YOU EVEN GET IN THERE? WELL, HANG TIGHT AND I—
UH
POIT
POIT
POIT

AAAHH NO NO NO
PLOP
yes!
DON'T WORRY I'VE GOT-
YOU

NOPE.
NOPE.
NOPE.
NOPE.
NOPE.
NOPE.
SOON
IT'S EMPTY...
UP4 GRABS
MEW
YOU COULD'VE SAID SOMETHING!
END

JE NE SAIS QUOI

MEREDITHMCCLAREN

UGH...THIS JOB WAS THE WORST...AND WHY DO THESE ALIENS KEEP STARING AT ME?

CLICK

AUG
GHH
HHH
HHH
HHH!

I CANNOT BE SEEN IN THIS ANYMORE!

PUPPYCAT.

PUPPYCAT.

PUPPYCAT.

HELP ME.

GUH?
< THIS IS WHERE WE KEEP ALL THE RETIRED OUTFITS. >

< MAYBE THERE'S ONE HERE YOU'LL LIKE. >

CAN PEOPLE ACTUALLY MOVE IN THIS?
UH. OH.
ABSOLUTELY NOT!

NONE OF THESE OUTFITS ARE REASONABLE!

THIS IS THE LAST ONE LEFT.

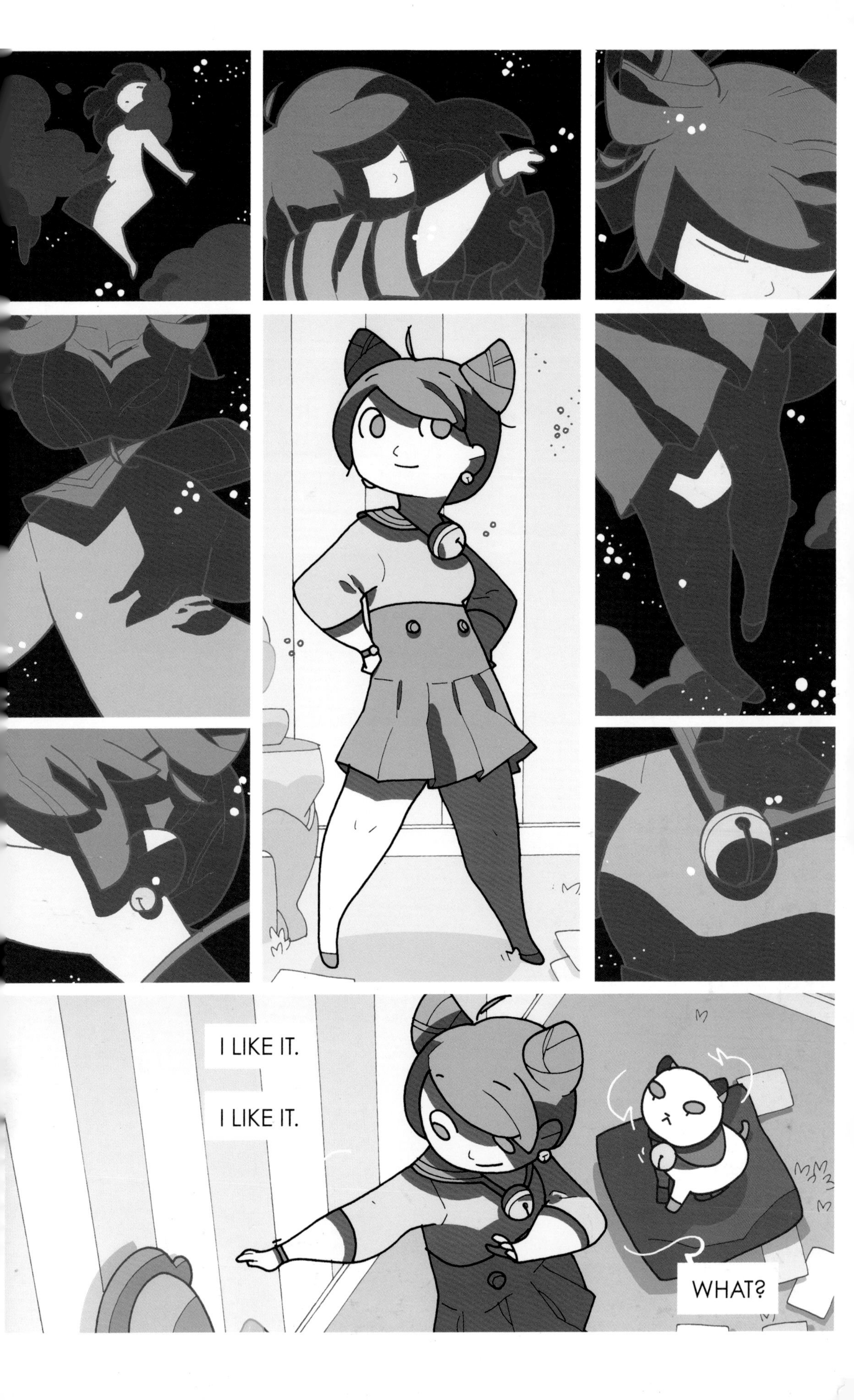
I LIKE IT.
I LIKE IT.
WHAT?

ARE WE SHORT ON TIME OR-?

THAT...
THAT TOOK TWO HOURS TO MAKE UP.

AND SO

SIGH.

END

By Andrew Lorenzi
BOOK QUEST

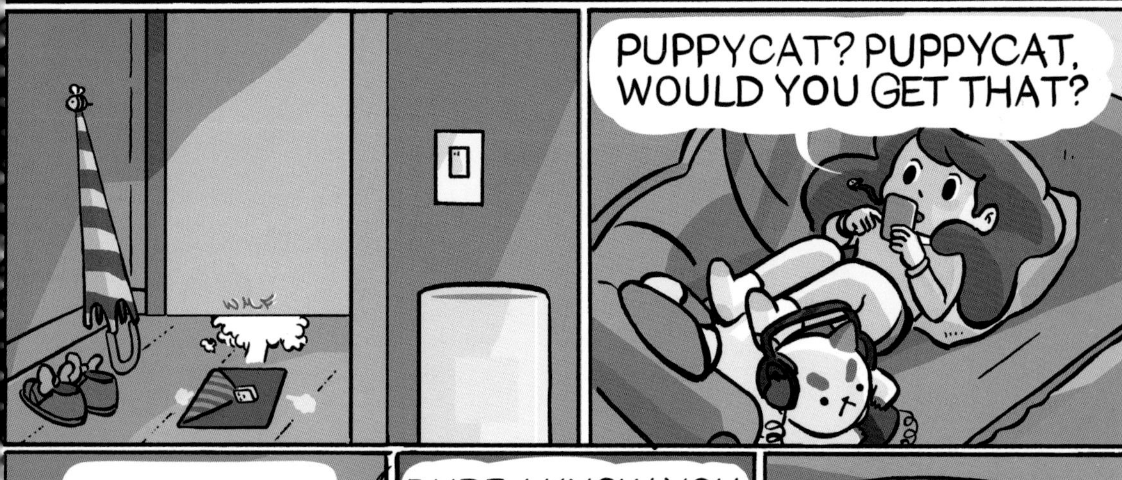
WMF
PUPPYCAT? PUPPYCAT, WOULD YOU GET THAT?

PUPPYCAT?

DUDE, I KNOW YOU CAN HEAR ME.

FINE! BE A BUTTCAT.

BUT IF I'VE WON A SWEEPSTAKES YOU'RE NOT SEEING ANY OF THAT PAPER..!

OH! LOOK! A BIG LETTER FROM THE PUBLIC LIBRARY. I BET IT'S A CHECK FOR A MILLION DOLLARS.

AUCH

<WHAT IS IT??>

AHHHH... I THINK I LOST A LIBRARY BOOK
...AND I WAS ALREADY STACKING UP CRAZY FINES...

STUPID ONLINE GAMING...
The following materials are overdue:
"THE UNOFFICIAL GUIDE TO WAR WIZARDRY"
Failure to return will result
suspension of your borrow

<THE LIBRARY? IS THAT WHERE YOU GET THOSE BOOKS YOU LEAVE AROUND THE BATHROOM?>

YES, *KYOTO ACADEMY 7*. I'VE READ ALL 154 ISSUES. IT WAS JUST STARTING TO GET GOOD.

AND IF I DON'T FIND THIS BOOK, I'LL BE BANNED FROM THE LIBRARY...
FOREVER..!

<OH.>

AND I WON'T BE ABLE TO CHECK OUT ANY MORE CDS FOR YOU...

<OH...>

<WELL, LET'S START LOOKING! IT COULDN'T TAKE THAT LONG TO SEARCH THIS PLACE.>

YEAAAHHH...

WHERE IS THIS BOOK??

I GIVE UP. IT'S NOT HERE.
AT LEAST IT'S NOT A TOTAL LOSS: I DID FIND THIS OLD CANDY.
<IF IT'S NOT HERE, WE MUST HAVE LEFT IT AT A RECENT JOB, RIGHT? YOU DON'T REALLY GO ANYWHERE ELSE...>
HM, TRUE.
SO, SHOULD WE JUST RETRACE OUR STEPS, OR...
<WE SHOULD CONSULT THE LEDGER OF INVOICES>
???
<...THAT NOTEBOOK...>
OOH! RIGHT.
OH, MAAAN, WE'VE BEEN ALL OVER THE GALAXY THIS MONTH
<BEE, THE SOONER WE START LOOKING...>
<THE SOONER WE CAN CHECK OUT MORE CDS>
<AND MANGA>
DEAL!

HEY, GUYS...FEELING ALRIGHT?

NO, I JUST SPENT MY DAY OFF ROOTING THROUGH SPACE, GETTING FILTHY AND KICKED AROUND

...PUPPYCAT'S TICKED OFF AT ME...

...ALL BECAUSE I LOST A DUMB LIBRARY BOOK.

DO YOU MEAN, "THE UNOFFICIAL GUIDE TO WAR WIZARDRY?"

YEAP. WHY, WERE YOU ON HOLD FOR IT? THEN I HAVE BAD NEWS FOR YOU...

BEE, YOU LENT ME THAT BOOK LAST WEEK. REMEMBER?

TEMP-BOT, I WOULD HAVE REMEMBERED TH--

UNOFFICIAL GUIDE TO WAR WIZARDRY

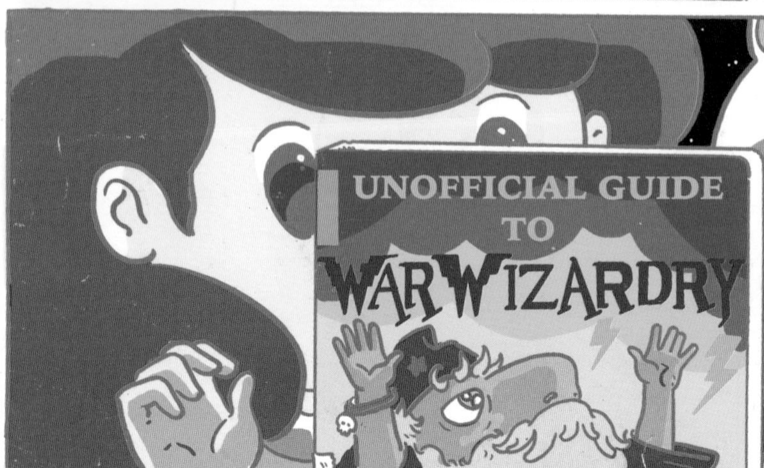
UNOFFICIAL GUIDE TO
WAR WIZARDRY

OKAY: WE'LL GROVEL FOR FORGIVENESS AND MAYBE THEY'LL BE LENIENT...
<DEAL>

OH, I APOLOGIZE! WE MEANT TO CALL YOU!

WE JUST ACQUIRED THE NEW EDITION OF THIS TITLE!

NORMALLY WE DISCARD THE OLD ONE, SO...

YOU'RE WELCOME TO KEEP IT!

UNOFFICIAL GUIDE TO
LEVEL UP!

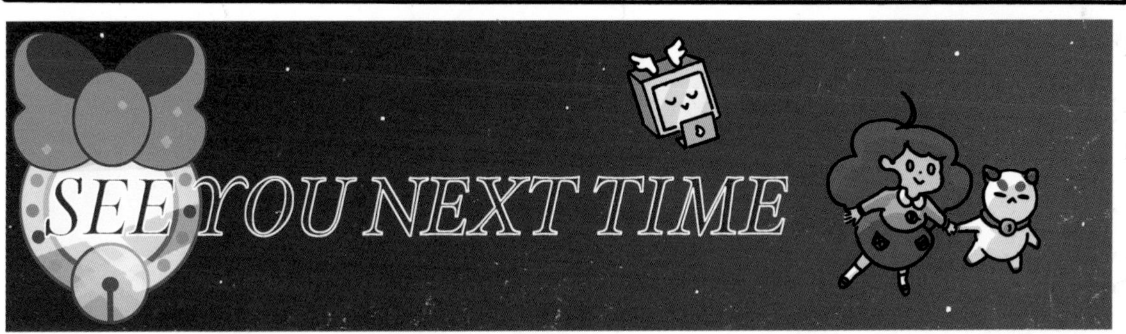
SEE YOU NEXT TIME

"Food"

Written & Illustrated by Joy Ang

Letters by Ashley Ang

ANOTHER TEMP JOB...

...COMPLETED!

WUMP

PUPPYCAT, CAN YOU GET OFF ME...
<I'M TRYING.>

PLUP
WHAT WAS THAT?

I GUESS WE GOT A PRESENT INSTEAD OF MONEY THIS TIME?

CUTE PACKAGING~

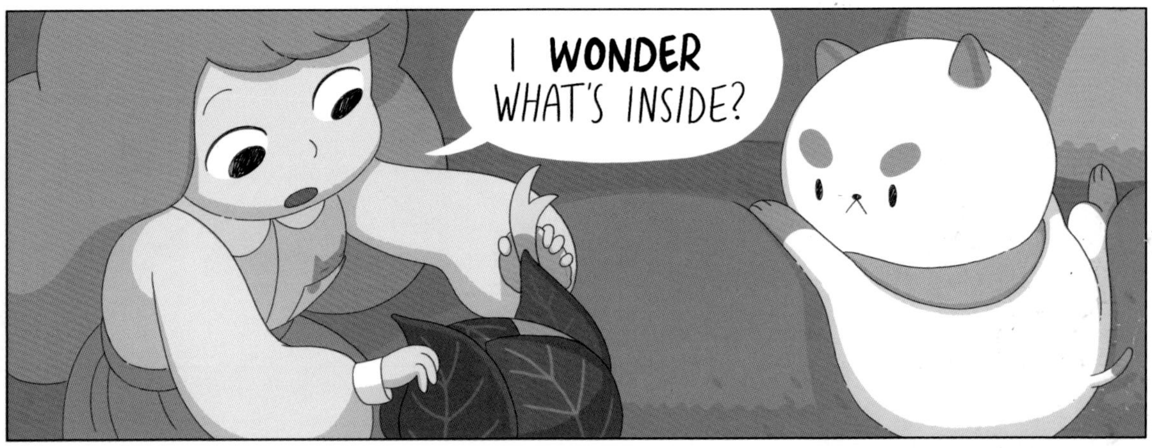
I **WONDER** WHAT'S INSIDE?

OH.

GLOOP

IT'S...
... A SQUISHY BLOBBY THING?

< THERE'S A NOTE. >

< IT SAYS TO PLACE YOUR HAND ON IT AND TO THINK OF WHATEVER FOOD YOU DESIRE. >

I DESIRE SO MANY FOODS...

SCHLOOP

AAHHH!
LOOK AT ALL THIS FOOD!

GET.
IN.
MY BELLY.

OH HEY, WHAT DID YOU GET?

SOMETHING... REALLY TINY?

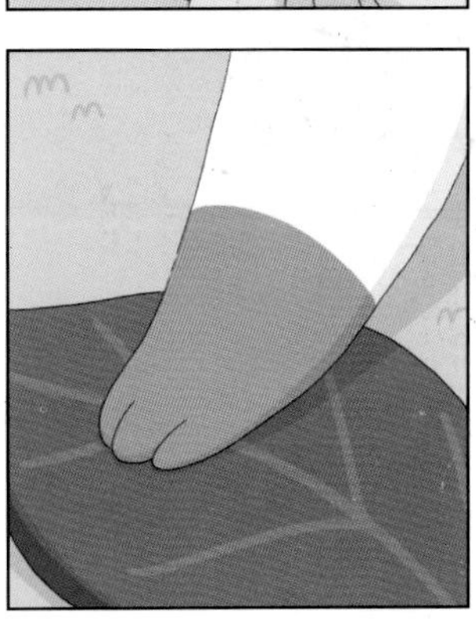

NOTHING

OH... LAME.
I GUESS I'LL SHARE...

HM?

< IT'S A SOUP MADE OF FLOATING SNOLS, SWEET GOLDEN JELLY, TENDER GREENS, SEARED FLUUGS, AND LENVISH EGGS. >

< EVERYTHING IS SEASONED WITH THE ESSENCE OF THE **SOULS FROM TEN THOUSAND INNOCENTS**. >

SERVED MEREDITH MCCLAREN

COCO
SQUEEK

101

SQUEEK
SQUEEK
SQUEEK
SQUEEK
SQUEEK
SQUEEK
SQUEEK
SQUEEK
SQUEEK
SQUEEK
SQUEEK
SQUEEK
SQUEEK
SQUEEK
SQUEEK
SQUEEK
SQUEEK
SQUEEK
SQUEEK
SQUEEK
SQUEEK
SQUEEK
SQUEEK
SQUEEK
SQUEEK
SQUEEK
SQUEEK
SQUEEK

SQUEEK
SQUEEK
SQUEEK
SQUEEK
SQUEEK
SQUEEK

BOOM!

SQUEEK

BEE AND PUPPYCAT IN: IMPROVISATION BY CAREY PIETSCH

BEE AND PUPPYCAT IN:
YES. YES IT IS.
BY CAREY PIETSCH

HELLO, PUPPYCAT!
HEY, TEMPS.
HELLO... GUEST.

WE HAVE A VERY SPECIAL JOB TODAY!
WHAT IS IT, TEMPBOT?
IT'S PERFORMANCE REVIEW DAY!

PLEASE COMPLETE YOUR PACKETS AND RETURN THEM TO ME.

BLEEEEEEAAAUUUU—

<DONE.>

WHAAAT? THIS IS LIKE A BAJILLION PAGES!
HOW THE HECK ARE YOU FINISHED?!

?

REVIEW
WHO'S A GOOD PUPPYCAT?
IS IT YOU?!
NO
YES

SHRUG.
THE END!

BEE AND PUPPYCAT IN: 5-STAR SPOT
BY CAREY PIETSCH
DECKARD!
DECK–MMF–HEY!

BEE! WHAT'S UP?
PUPPYCAT FOUND THIS GREAT NEW FOOD TRUCK.
C'MON!

HUH. AREN'T THEY USUALLY ALL OUT BY THE LIBRARY...?
THOSE LINES ARE WAY TOO LONG.
CHECK THIS OUT:

TA-DAHHH!!!
THIS IS AN ABANDONED PICKUP.
ISN'T IT GREAT? THEY'RE TOTALLY FREE!
YOU GOTTA TRY ONE!

ehhhhhhhhhhhhhhhhhhh–

SHOVE

CHEW
CHEW

THIS...

THIS IS THE BEST TACO I'LL EVER HAVE.
THE END!

BEE AND PUPPYCAT IN: MAGICALLY DELICIOUS?
BY CAREY PIETSCH

HEY PUPPYCAT, WHAT'S–
<HERE!>

<TEMP–BOT WANTED ME TO BRING HOME THESE BOOKS.>
<SOMETHING ABOUT READING UP ON THE HISTORY OF YOUR PROFESSION.>
HOW'D YOU GET TO THE LIBRARY ALL BY YOURSELF?

UH. SARA TROTTER AND THE ENCHANTED FIRE PIT?
SARA TROTTER

THE WITCH who BARBECUED TOO much
Fire SPELLS, COOKOUTS, & YOU
SORCEROUS KEBABS OF THE 20TH century
FANTASTIC CHARCOAL and where to FIND IT
PUPPYCAT, WHAT ARE THESE?!
DING

PUPPYCAT: TYPO IN PREVIOUS INSTRUCTIONS. CORRECTED LIST OF BOOKS TO FOLLOW.
-T.B.

???

<OH.>
<NOT MAGICAL GRILLS.>
HA HA HA HA!
GURGLLL

GROWLLLL

BUT LET'S HANG ON TO ONE OR TWO, JUST IN CASE.
THE END!

by Andrew Lorenzi

SEE YOU NEXT TIME, TEMP-BOT!
<I AM SO TIRED... I'M GOING TO NAP FOR A FEW DAYS.>
WELL, ACTUALLY... THERE'S SOMEWHERE I WANTED TO TAKE YOU FIRST.

<PLEASE, BEE. MY LEGS ARE MUCH SMALLER THAN YOURS.
I'M EXHAUSTED.>

I PROMISE IT'LL BE SUPER FUN! JUST A *TINY* DETOUR.

<*GROAN*>
<PLEASE. JUST BE QUICK, THEN.>

IT'LL BE GREAT.

<WHAT IS THIS PLACE?>
2 cute 2 poot

< WHY ARE THERE SO MANY HUMANS CONGREGATING HERE? >

IT'S THE AUTUMN CARNIVAL!
<...IT SMELLS LIKE FRIED FOODS.>

WAY CHEAPER THAN A MOVIE, SUPER FUN RIDES...

...AND ALL THE FOOD IS FRIED!

<BEE... HELP>

LET ME GIVE YOU THE TOUR.

TICKETS!

FOOD!

PETTING ZOO

...WAITING...

RIDES!

...PRIZES...

OH

MY

GOSH

I NEED THAT KOALA CLOCK

IT'S PERFECT.

HOW MUCH??
FIVE BUCKS FOR THREE THROWS

<BEE. WHAT ARE YOU DOING ?>

I'M TAKING HOME THAT KOALA.

CHECK THIS OUT

WOOMF

BONK

OOF.
TOUGH LUCK.

<HERE.
I'VE GOT IT.>

WOOOOSH

BUNK

WHOOPS.
IT LOOKS LIKE
OUR LITTLE KITTY
IS A WEAKLING,
TOO.

PUPPYCAT.
THE BALL.
PLEASE.

BOOM

FSSSsss

THWK

YES! YES!
KOALA CLOCK!
KO-A-LA CUH-LOCK!

ALRIGHT,
PUPPYCAT!

JUST ONE MORE STO--

...!

PUPPYCAT! OUR KOALA HAS BEEN KIDNAPPED!!

<THERE!>
HALL OF MIRR

STOP!

TICKETS, PLEASE.
OH, COME *ON.*

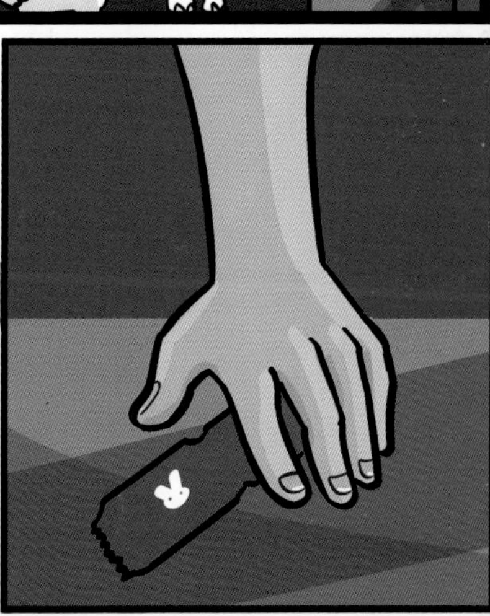

ENJOY...
I *WILL.*

WOW, UHM, THIS IS KIIINDA SPOOKY.

<THIS IS NOTHING! IT'S JUST A SERIES OF MIRRORS ARRANGED IN-->

HA HA HA HA
HEH HEH

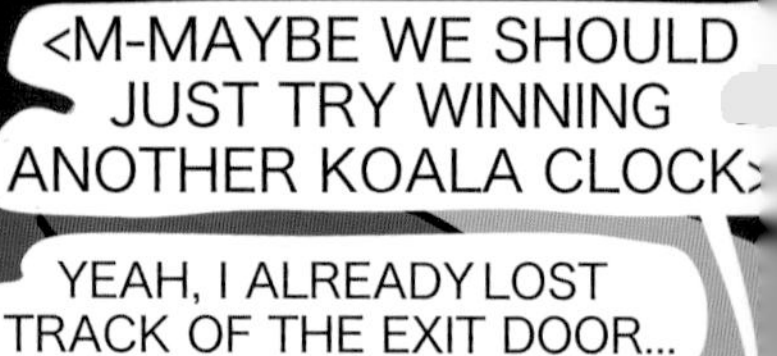
<M-MAYBE WE SHOULD JUST TRY WINNING ANOTHER KOALA CLOCK>

YEAH, I ALREADY LOST TRACK OF THE EXIT DOOR...

HEY, *THIEF* ! KEEP THE CLOCK! HIS IMPECCABLE TIMEKEEPING IS YOURS!

DING DING DING DING DIN
??

G DING DIN
<WAIT>

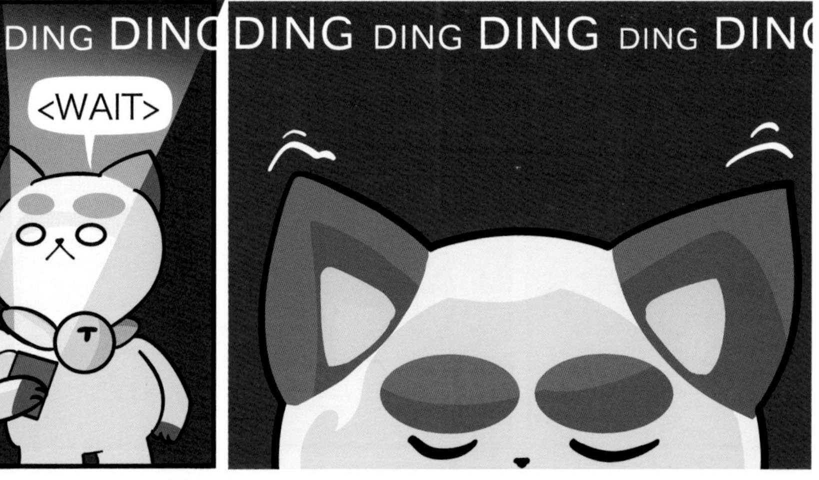
DING DING DING DING DIN

HEY!

!
ING DING

A KID?
...YOU STOLE... WHY?

I TRIED WINNING IT ALL DAY, BUT... I COULDN'T AND... ...I JUST WANTED IT.
...

I'M SORRY

PUPPYCAT, GIVE HER THE CLOCK.

<BEE, ARE YOU SURE?>

I'M SURE. I WANT HER TO HAVE IT.

WELL, WHAT NOW?

OH, I DID WANT TO DO ONE MORE THING. BUT, I UNDERSTAND IF YOU WANT TO GET HOME.

<NO, NO. I'M FINE. WHAT DID YOU HAVE IN MIND?>

<BEE, THAT WAS NICE OF YOU TO GIVE AWAY YOUR CLOCK.>

YEAH, IT'S A NICE CLOCK...

...BUT I ONLY REALLY WANTED IT SO I WOULDN'T FORGET TODAY.

END

"Gardening"
Written & Illustrated by
Zachary Sterling
Letters by
Mad Rupert
GARDEN SHOP

THANKS AGAIN FOR HELPING ME PICK OUT SOME SEEDS...
NO PROBLEM! I JUST CAN'T WAIT TO SEE WHAT KINDS OF THINGS YOU'LL BE ABLE TO COOK ONCE THEY GROW!

OH LOOK!

WHOA.

SEED STATION
IT'S SO PRETTY...

SO, WHAT'RE YOU GONNA GROW?
I-I DON'T KNOW!
THERE'S SO MANY OF THEM...

DON'T WORRY, WE'LL PICK THEM FOR YOU!

NOW LET'S SEE HERE...
OH!

I LIKE THIS ONE!

<THIS ONE IS GOOD.>

SOME TOMATOES AND SUGAR-SNAP PEAS!

<THESE ARE ALSO GOOD.>

UH... DO YOU GUYS THINK THAT'S ENOUGH--

YES.
<NO.>
LATER...
SO, WHICH ONE DO WE PLANT FIRST?
WHY DON'T WE JUST DO A LITTLE BIT OF EACH?
PAT
PAT
PAT
PAT
PAT
GOOD LUCK, LITTLE SEEDS.

WHEW! IT MAY HAVE BEEN A LOT OF HARD WORK...
BUT IT'S TOTALLY GONNA BE WORTH IT!
I'M GONNA TRY TO COOK SO MANY THINGS ONCE IT ALL GROWS!
THERE'S SO MANY THINGS YOU'LL BE ABLE TO MAKE TONIGHT...

A STRAWBERRY DECORATION CAKE!

AND PUMPKIN PIE!

OR SOME CORN CAKES!
CORNBREAD!

TONIGHT? BEE, IT'S GOING TO TAKE MONTHS BEFORE ANYTHING GROWS.

BUT...I'M HUNGRY NOW!
END

Sick Day! (by Megan Brennan)

Well, we did it Puppycat.

We made it through the whole monster movie marathon. We sat through 12 hours of guys in rubber suits knocking cardboard buildings over. We can do anything now.
Pat

DING DONG!
!!
CLATTER

Hey Bee, I was just dropping off this DVD I borrowed-

Wow are you okay? you look sick!

uhhh... we were kinda up all night watching movies, I'm totally worn out

Hey, even if you aren't sick, I make a great chicken noodle soup. It might make you feel a little better! You know. If you want.

That would be SO GREAT!
I'll bring the soup and DVD by once I get off work!
Finally, being an unemployed slob is paying off! I can't wait to try that soup!
SLAM!
Okay buddy, we've got a little time to practice looking REALLY cute-
Oh nooo Puppycat, right NOW?
I'm sooo tired from that movie marathon. You know, maybe that wasn't a great idea after all-
Hey there new hires! We're so glad you're joining us today at Candy Conglomerate! We hope you have a sweet day helping us out at the factory!
Please sort the candy into boxes, place the sealed boxes on the conveyor-
Maybe this won't be so bad!

Now, we know it is tempting, but we must insist that you do NOT try the candy, if it is consumed by those from another dimension we cannot guarantee-
Eating the candy is not compliant with company policy.
oh...okay
Puppycat we've totally got this, I mean, we ate like 5 pounds of candy last night. Candy is our LIFE.
Yeah...we are in our ELEMENT...
ZZZZZ
!
!
tap tap
AAAAH!!
We have to finish this job now, I can't stay late to fix this, I have to go home and hang out with Deckard!

if there's one thing I know how to do, it's how to make candy disappear!
it tastes kinda weird. like spicy...grass? But I'm not gonna let that stop me!
I can't believe how much of that stuff I ate. Good going with putting the rest in boxes though, buddy-
EXIT
Sneeaak
I guess technically you finished a day of work but-
ACHOO!
ugh... I can't get that candy taste out of my mouth...
Whew! Back with time to spare before Deckard arrives!
Bonk!

it's naaaaaaaaptime! Gotta sleep off all that weird space candy...
Pat Pat
Z Z Z Z Z
Ding Dong!
!!
ACHOOO!
Man, maybe they were right when they said not to eat that candy, after all.
KNOCK KNOCK!
I don't feel so great-

Heeyyyyy
Here you go, my famous soup! Looks like you really need it.
If you're feeling up to it, I heard there's a Bird Detectives marathon on today. We can watch together if you want?
glug
glug
glug

Yeah, totally!!

AND SO:
ZZZ
Bird! Detective!
THE END!

"Pancoma"
Written & Illustrated by
T. Zysk
yawn
What a beautiful day...
It feels like a day for accomplishment...
Today...
I want to eat a lot of pancakes.
<Don't you have any better life goals?>
$$$
Hm...
All these pancakes are so expensive...
How can people afford this??
bmp

Ee! Oh! Puppycat!
I thought you didn't want to eat pancakes with me!
Did you change your mind?
Oh!! Look at that one!
ALL U CAN EET CHEAP PANCAKS
I bet we can afford that!
<...>
Pancakes here we come!
<It's not worth it! Bee!>

Oh-
sscootchh
Oh hey there. You lookin for pancakes?
<Bee this guy's got my hackles up! I didn't even know I had hackles!>
Er... Is this a restaurant or...?
Nah pal, but if you're lookin for pancakes, I gotcha covered.
SYRUP
Not interested in pancakes?!
You a cop?!
EE!!
EEP!!
Uh... I think I made a mistake...
<I told you so!>
You're here to bust my counterfeit pancake operation, aren't you?!
SWSSH

Well it's not gonna happen pal !!
No one's gonna take down Old Stacks !!
!!
Puppycat... What happened?
<You complained about how expensive it was but then you came in anyway and ordered 12 pancakes. And then presumably fell into some sort of pancake coma.>
A... panCOMA...
Here's your bill.
<nom nom>
END

"Sweaters"
Written & Illustrated by
T. Zysk
Puppycat?
Eyy, have you seen my blue sweater?
Puppycat?
Oh, there it is!
grab
Hey! My clothes are not a bed!
scoot
<MINE!>
thnk

ff
There! You're way too short to get them up here.
<Bee, I will call the police!>
Just go use the pillows I gave you, you baby!
Honestly I don't know what is up with pets and clothes.
<Not a pet!>
I can't walk around with fur all over my clothes! people will think I have an animal relationship with weird boundaries!
<You do though.>
Believe me, this is better for both of-

H-how did you even!?!?
<Not a pet.>
floof
Spin
thunk
This is over.

The next morning...
yawn
Puppycat?
Huh.
Probably still
mad at me.
clik
clik
EH?!!
Z
Z
I-it's...
impossible...
At least he's
cute in there...
sigh
END

"Snapshots"

Written & Illustrated by David Calderon

DREAM ON

VROOM

VROOM
VROOM

Z z z z

Z z z z

VROOM
VROOM

Z z z z z

Z z z z z

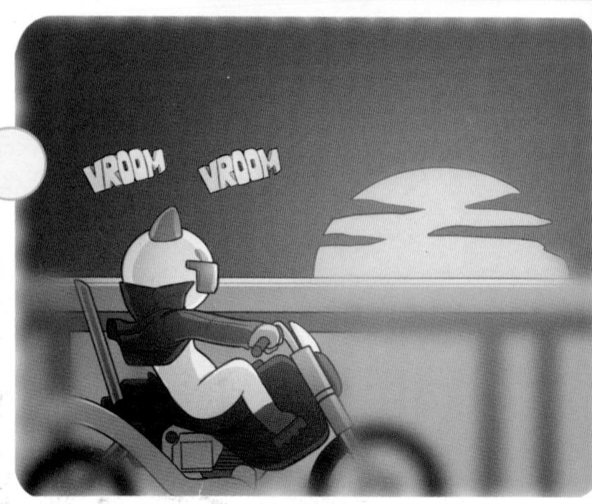
VROOM
VROOM

THE LAST

< QUICKLY! >

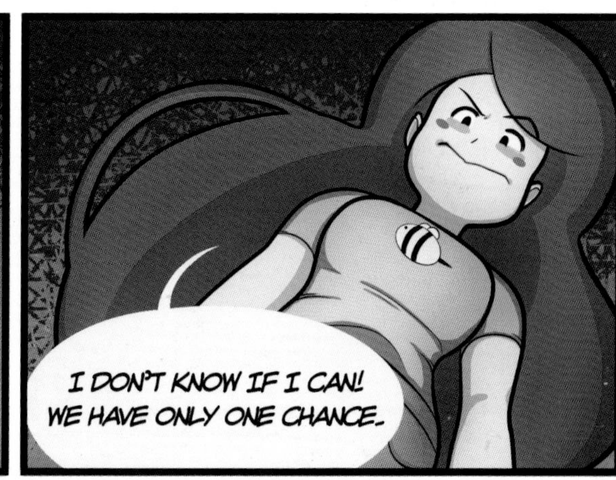
I DON'T KNOW IF I CAN! WE HAVE ONLY ONE CHANCE...

< YOU CAN! >

BUT IT'S...
< DO IT! >

...THE LAST CHOCOLATE BAR!!

IT'S VERY HARD TO CUT INTO TWO EQUAL PARTS...
END

"Bubbles"

Written & Illustrated by

Liz Fleming

POP
AGH! WHAT IS THAT NOISE?
POP
<AHHHHHHHHHHHHHH>
POP
POP
YEAH, THAT'S NOT HELPING!
POP
WELL, WHATEVER IT IS, IT'S WAY LOUDER DOWNSTAIRS...
CARDAMON?
PUPPYCAT?

DON'T DO THAT.
PUPPYCAT!! STOP BEIN' RUDE!

CARDAMON, WHAT ARE YOU EVEN DOING OUT HERE?
WE HAVE TO LEARN HOW TO PLAY THE RECORDER FOR SCHOOL. SO I'M PRACTICING.
OH.... COOL, BUT, CAN'T YOU TRY TO PRACTICE A LITTLE SOFTER?
NO.

MY BUBBLES!
<PUT THAT THING DOWN RIGHT NOW TINY HUMAN OR I'LL->

BWOOOOOP
WHA-
CARDAMON!! STOP TOOTIN'!!
YOU'RE GONNA FLY AWAY!!

OH WOW!!

POP
HA HA! HOW IS THIS HAPPENING?
<BEAUTIFUL>
HEY CARDAMON! ISN'T THIS GREA-
C-CARDAMON?
WELL, I'VE MASTERED THE RECORDER, SO I'M GONNA GO BACK INSIDE NOW.
<YOU HAVEN'T LEARNED A THING!!>
AW MAN... MY BUBBLES.
THE END

o No Nooo
Pic Pic Pic
DECKARD WILL BE SO SAD IF I DON'T GET THESE CRUSTIES OFF THE PAN HE LENT ME!
SLAP!
MON MON
C'MON
STUPID MEATLOAF.
RAHHH!!
PWI PWI BOooo
I CAN'T CALL CARDAMON! ARE YOU NUTS?!
excuse me
HELLO HI, CARDAMON? YEAAAAAA I HAVE AN EMERGENCY.
LATER
WHAT IS YOUR EMERGENCY?
HELLLPP MEEE I CAN'T GET THIS MEATLOAF OFFFF
THAT IS NOT AN EMERGENCY!
AIEE! CARDAMON NO!
"Tubberware"
xoxo COLEMAN ENGLE

Bee & Puppycat in
"The Blues"
urghhh
grooooan
mhhh!
@#!!∞
How are you going to be a responsible adult if you can't get out of bed??
mnggh puppycat, not nowww
But you've things to do
shove!
Go awayyy... feelin' real bad right now... SO tired
ARGH
Stupid lazy human! I don't know how her civilisation lasted 5000 years

Time to fix this ridiculous problem!
woaaaaaayhn!
How can I help you, Puppycat?
My work partner has been incapacitated by a kind of general malaise that is associated with mood swings.
Ah! I know just the thing!
hello hello
frump
welcome to...

DEVON'S
artificially
CONSTRUCTED
magical FUN
CARNIVAL!

You've NO idea how long we've been waiting for hired help (days, months, etc)

We're a lil' short on, ah
manpower

So you gotta help us with a few odd jobs around here Nothing TOO hard!

Oooo good job! Time for your
PAY
finally

Choc

what even...
hehe~ see you soon~

Not only are they seriously understaffed, they exploit animals with toxic foods...
Choc
Hey!
Oh hey Puppycat! Deckard's been caring for me real swell! He even made *CHOCOLATE*
munch
I'm feeling way better now!
MMMMMMMAAAAAAAAAAA
Maybe he's getting sick?
AAAAAAAAAHHHHHH

END

cover gallery

Issue Five Cover by Emily Hu

Issue Five Cover by Zac Gorman

Issue Five Variant Cover by Emily Partridge

Issue Six Cover by Caroline Breault

Issue Six Cover by Natalie Nourigat

Issue Six Variant Cover by Zac Gorman

Issue Seven Cover by Felicia Choo

Issue Seven Cover by Brian Fukushima

Issue Seven Variant Cover by Geneva Hodgson

Issue Eight Cover by Hwei Lim

Issue Eight Cover by Mady Martin

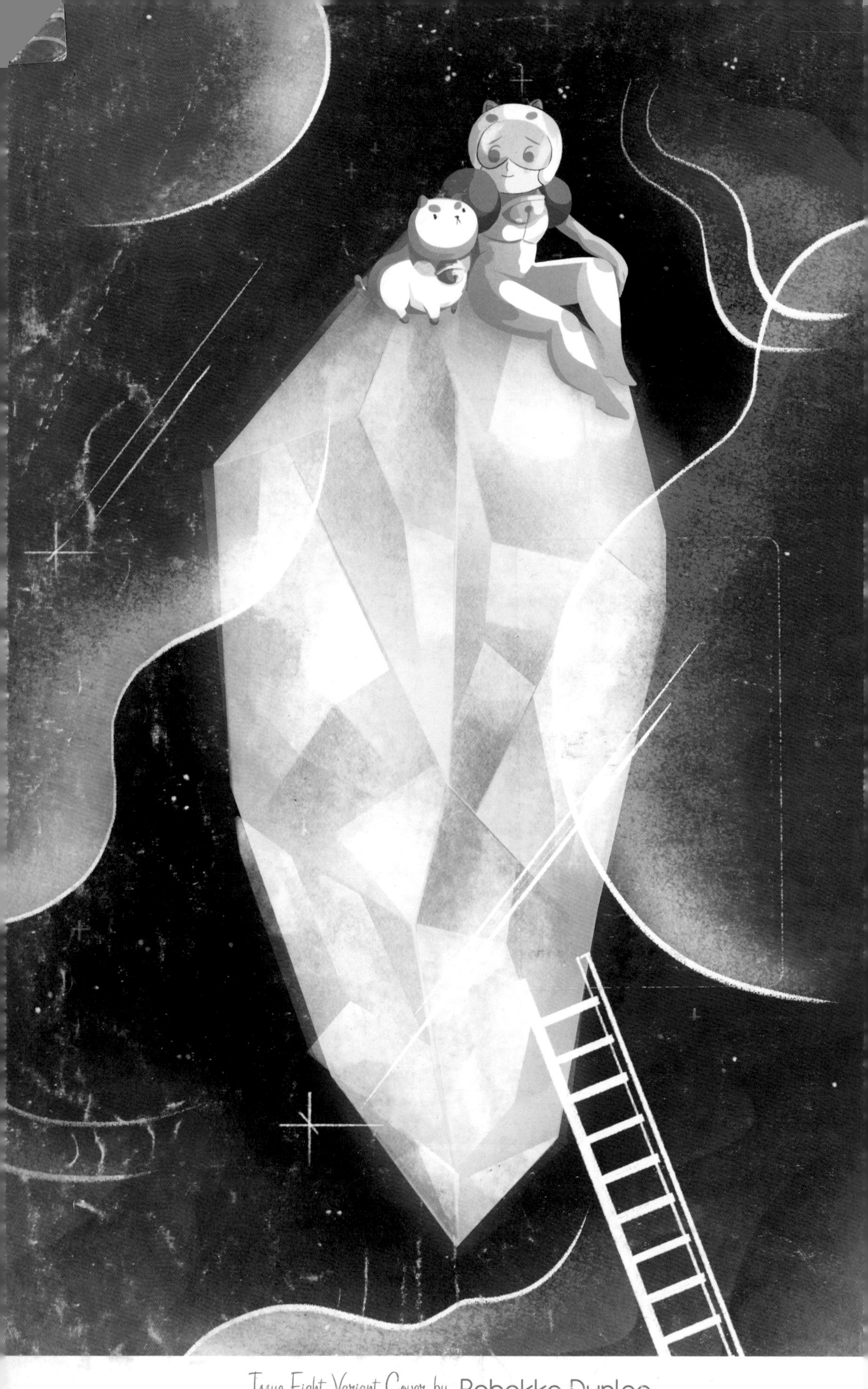

Issue Eight Variant Cover by Rebekka Dunlap